THE WEATHER COMING

CW01046250

For Rachel and Nicola

Annemarie Austin

THE WEATHER COMING

TAXVS

ACKNOWLEDGEMENTS:
Acknowledgements are due to **Agenda, Argo, The Green Book**, Mandeville Press, **National Poetry Competition Anthology 1985, New Poetry 8** (Arts Council/Hutchinson), **Other Poetry, Poems 82** (Lancaster Literature Festival), **Poetry Durham, Poetry Now** (BBC Radio 3), **Prospice, Sotheby's International Poetry Competition Anthology 1982, South West Review**, Starwheel Press, **Sunday Telegraph Magazine** and **Writing Women** where some of these poems first appeared

ISBN 1 85019 045 3

First published 1987 by
TAXVS PRESS
Stamford Arts Centre,
27 St. Mary's Street,
Stamford,
Lincolnshire PE9 2BN.

Set by Taxus Press
and printed at The Russell Press,
Bertrand Russell House, Nottingham NG7 4ET

CONTENTS

THE LONG UNDRESSING

(Walter de la Mare: 'They say death's a
going to bed; I doubt it, but anyhow
life's a long undressing.')

I left a ribbon of skin along the stairs tonight.
I lie beside you in the bed and think of it:
it shines like a snail's trail under the moon through
   the skylight
and seems more precious off than on me;
stopped in its life it somehow turns to art.

This is the way it goes, the long undressing.
Oh how we shed ourselves in eyelashes, nail clippings.
They fall to patterns in the wet bottom of the bath
— collages and found poems — surrendered almost
   wantonly:
the curious prodigality of living.

Age thins us, lips and shins. Our shoulder blades grow
into wings, but there can be no flying while we wade
through this detritus, garments slipping from the
   bedroom chair.
Unlock the desk, unclose a folded, faded envelope:
my white-blonde childhood hair curls in a snailshell
   spiral.

POSTCARD OF RIMBAUD
IN A DREAM OF AFRICA

A black foot, walking, disturbs a yellow stone.
There, in its shadow, the shed skin of a snake —
dry, curled and near transparent, faintly splotched.

The postcard of Rimbaud as a poet of sixteen
— oval of sepias on a cream oblong — lies
on its back, pitched through a blank letter slot.

The sixteen porters, hired from Harar to Zeilah,
gather and hoist a stretcher to shoulder height.
The body they carry has this picture for a face:

blurred as if by the speed of their going, hair
tousled one way by wind, tie as though blown
in the other. The eyes look past a long way,

waiting for this desert it will take
twelve days to cross . . . . The postcard floats
on the horizontal, dividing sky and ground.

The distant gaze is fixed on a lack of cloud
and white-hot sun to be looked at only sidelong.
Under the paper rectangle: a lion-coloured earth

and yellow grass, untiring feet stepping on,
the flicker of a lizard going, track of
the sidewinder snake across the dunes.

From hospital Rimbaud wrote to his family
of being flayed . . . . here on the card is his
    shed skin
faintly splotched, the near-transparent poet
    put aside.

FLASHER

He did not look for the faces —
to see and enjoy the sudden shock
or whatever the eyes and mouths would suggest;
it was the train he was showing himself to,
by the side of the track, hair wild on the edge
of the slipstream, his jacket flapping back;
it was the train, wiping out specific vision
with its speed, so that he could not anyway
look at faces, perceive the astonished Os
of the mouths; the train, on its horizontal way
through his head, blasting it open from ear to ear
with the rushing and rushing, the flashing and
    flashing
of window then window then window in the sun.

GWEN JOHN AT DIEPPE

After the train
and its rushing outside the ears,
its shaking and stirring of clothes and bones —
the world gone grainy, painted on flying chaff,
a humming against the lid of the brain,
fires in the ears,
the dark.

Cliffs the colour of mustard.
Stomach starved to a child's fist size.
Beds in lines, white, starched.

White falls apart, to starch grains or to snow.
Ever quieter in the attic, a small child sings alone.
Bonfires along the cliff are put out, one by one.

JACOBEAN

Dark wood. A face without eyelashes
looks at me sidelong, lying upon its ruff.
Barbaric colours beneath: the blood and black.

Long-fingered hand curves on the polished skull,
familiar as a breast, as pale in shadows
scarfing the figure. Death comes

with the book kissed, the nosegay smelt,
is brought in a basket of cooling apricots.
Head on a platter stares out of night alive.

HOLLAND UNCOLOURED, 1949

The son of our hosts has no hair, no eyebrows.
In the hotel's narrow loft he hid out the Occupation,
barefoot above the heads of billeted soldiers,
padding a vigil. Of a sudden, four years on,
his wild orange locks have fallen.
His armpits are now as white and sleek
as the membraned insides of eggshells.

The Rijksmuseum Rembrandts dazzle with varnish.
A hand, a blurred pale face floats to the surface
like the gas-buoyed drowned. 'The Night Watch',
in its room alone, compels my anxious motion
back and forth, bringing figures out of blackness.
My mother copies the catalogued pictures for me.
I prefer her pencilled version, grey on white.

VISITING THE ANGEL

Winter. No-colour colours. A bruise-shadowed sea
beats in. The churchyard hangs above it,
crammed with grey box-shaped tombs.

Father and daughter come there in their
sensible dark clothes, padded against the weather,
find the angel scratched in slate lying awake.

Someone must have used a coin for outlining
its face, ready to spin across the graveyard
like a discus — or like the daughter's dream of flying

that she remembers now, her gloved hand on the round
    head
of the angel, holding it a moment in its place.
They climb down from the churchyard to the beach.

A strip of greyish-brown. A cold cliff scree.
Under a flat grey winter sky a greyer sea
beats in. They are the only figures.

He teaches her the tricks of skimming stones:
the choice of pebbles like fat coins,
the hanging stride, the sideswipe of the arm.

One hand ungloved, she tries and tries again
before her stones begin flatly to lift and skip
among the waves, flirting with broken surfaces.

The daughter greets familiarly that edge of air
between a dreaming pebble and its ground.
She watches little angels fly upon the tide.

ANCHORITE

The anchorite — kernel of a shut nut made of stone —
hearkens to birdsong filtering to him
from an imagined wood outside his wall.

Within the wood the soldier — ten years before
escaped from battle — watches amid massed leaves
the bird of separated parts singing upon a stone.

No song in the whirr of bullets past his ears.
When he returned at first each hill
was nothing but a crater upside down,

and he was flung into the air against it
like a four-winged bird whenever he walked there.
But time still flies, the air calms downward,

maelstroms subside, hills rise up to where they
  should.
The bird and he divide to sit apart — the watched
and watcher with a rapt, awakened face.

Massed leaves between them make green spaces in his
  skin.
He moves no more than stone. He is himself
an anchorite, forgetting any world outside his wall.

TEMPORARY LODGING

The front door's Yale lock opened
for the shallow curve of a sixpence —
we kept one under a stone in place of the key.

The gas tap beside the boarded-up fireplace
connected with somebody else's supply,
forever free-fuelling a stockpot for us.

The geyser long ago blew the bathroom window out.
In a sour row of dishes under the sideboard
my flatmate grew fungus on purpose.

Sometimes in the attic, a bright shadow
fumbled the handles of bedroom doors.
She stood once, her green dress
threaded by daylight, in the narrow kitchen
where the gas stove years before
had opened its reeking mouth to be her brief pillow.

THE DARKHOUSE

1.

It flowers up from the cellar-hole, clogged
with roots and boles, and overgrows the night air
of the hillside: an intenser darkness — there,
where great trees hold the shrub patterns
of a garden, its walks from nought to nought.

Not-structure looms. The un-house stands
within its pallisade of hawthorn hedge
grown rampant and long-fingered. Its lost
facade blacks out the hazy stars. A drift
of sheep avoids the thick of pointed gable shadow.

2.

There is a continent inside the dark:
an Africa of high and lowland,
forest, river basins, rock.
It moves under the moon
like cooling lava creeping or
a desert's rearrangement by the wind.

And has its creatures such as
galloping night mares, the dark horse
passing by with muffled hooves.
Every year the house cat gave birth
on a kitchen shelf; her kitten
ghosts fly down, fly down again.

THE BONE SHIP

Squinnying under my father's elbow, I saw the cow
inexorably sink in the bottomless, bottomless rhyne.
Men were urgent to raft her with bales of brushwood,
forking them under the unseen belly —
arms were gone to the shoulders in effort to lift;
but transition flood to mud in the cellar of the ditch
was no more than drifting particles casually changing
    places.
She bellowed one last time before seep of water
filled up her throat and her desperate nostrils
    bubbled.

I have her still and always in the black back of my
    mind.
She is a bone ship now and journeys beneath the
    surface
through the exact ditch grid, the willow-watched
    canals,
idly rocking on her spine keel, white ribs lifting
in the thick and sepia marsh-born liquid,
her horns the prongs of the vessel's slipped anchor.
She is a ghost craft for such as the Flying Dutchman
— gravity turns aside from her weight
as her bones ride the rhyne water.

WHITEWORK

The background to these poems is Sir John Franklin's
ill-fated expedition in search of the North-West
Passage. He and 128 others set out in June 1845 and
were never seen alive again. Some forty expeditions
searched for them in the decade from 1848.

'Whitework' is embroidery in white thread on the same
colour ground.

Child's Eye

1.

A monkey has gone with the ships,
they tell her.
      She recalls the below-deck she saw,
its shallow and tiny brown and blackness,
and conjures a monkey's life
as circumscribed as her own —
             knee-high to tables,
intimate as she is with the undersides of shelves,
the tails of coats and shiny sit-down marks
on breeches.
      Then the snow.
             The terrible dazzle
in brown, melancholy eyes. Ice underneath the fur.
The cabin, the circumscribed world once again,
constriction of sudden clothes meant to warm.

2.

Such a very busy cardboard and plaster Arctic:
beyond each iceberg like an oak tree or cathedral
a population follows polar bears, creeps up
on basking seals or meets a delegation from
the not-so-many native Eskimos. And ships —
the ships are everywhere like toys, their rigging
clearly sewing cotton.
                            I look for Father.
                                         Everyone
is splendid: white collars opened and thrown back,
they take the polar wind on naked throats;
it fans their hair and fills their undone coats
while Eskimos are fur to lips and eyebrows.
All profiles are identical, all face one way . . . .
I cannot recognise my memory of Father.

But dreams of ice and this ice are the same —
the caster-sugar castles, the cave mouths
fringed with daggers, skating lakes
and white and giant helter-skelter slides.

Whitework

1.

Putting out washing, she watches birds —
the sparrows wrangling. Their spurts of dust,
beak voices; and the white-sheet walls
hang down.
    Out of Woolwich the great ship's sails
were furled behind its tow ropes. It was a grid
of ribs and washing lines. And a white dove came
and settled on its mast-head.
    She remembers that,
the white dove on the mast-head, settled up above
the black-against-the-sky nest for the crow.

2.

A white cat crossed the cobbles
under the stable archway, and
she was transfixed by its ice-green eyes.
    She thought
of winter gulls on the inland fields like paper,
scattered.
    She thought
of the creatures where he was,
of the white wolves she had heard of,
great white bears that walk erect as men do,
white seabirds — like these but not like paper,
vanished upon the snow.

3.

The moon hung in the rectangle of her window
like a white, white stone. It cast its slab
of light onto the bed.

In the longboat mounted upon a sledge,
alongside the two skeletons, they found
the shipboard slippers she had worked for Jack,
binding the edges with red ribbon.

She watched the moon slide down the sky.
Its light weighed heavy on her breast and face.
One man had leaned his spade against a skull,
taking it for white stone.

The Ice-master's Wife

I.

The boys are gone into the big bed now.
This bed is narrow, narrow — a hot brick
wrapped in flannel crowds my side.
I lie here. I am waking.

A child stirs, cries out of his dream.
Along the alleyway the cats are courting . . . .

My mind ticks and lurches:
the whales jerk by;
blizzards, like looking down
on pots of curdled milk,
spill, spill into the dark . . . .

Under the window a cat screams
and I think of quiet —
                                    the way that snowfall muffles,
wraps around, the sound of shoes returning.

2.

In the light dissolved dark of summer
she dreamed of black winter dark
and frozen men slipped into frozen holes
like letters posted to the ground.
                                    Her boys
were gone for sailors too, and gone north
with the whalers as he'd done. Night
pressed around her, cold pressed around,
whatever the lift of the sun, the width
of the broad yellow flood across her floor.

What would they weight the eyelids with
in a land with no need for coins?

In her sleep she saw the indoor look
of heels and hands unlocked from boots and gloves.
They would tie the feet together, bind the arms
before he met the ground.
                          Then she woke
because light woke her. No carrier pigeons
back from the Arctic roosted among
the extravagant leaves of trees outside her window.

Voices

1.

I thought I had forgotten Harry
— his picture put away inside a drawer.
                                 But now
the terrible,
the terrible restores him.
The daguerreotype out again,
I look for his bones in his eyes.

                        Those bones perhaps
in the sledded boat with clothes and pounds of
   chocolate,
those bones of Harry's
sunken in snow, stirred by an accidental spade.

There was a white skull.
There was a pocket comb strung with brown hairs . . . .

His hair was brown.
                   I remember.

2.

I cannot somehow believe in a death undeclared
when the shelled peas fall, ringing softly,
into the china basin, when light from the whiteness
lifts to brim my features, and bruised pods scent the
    garden
over the odour of roses.
                                    I see instead:
                                                    Jack
in a strange polar summer
where daisies drive their heads up through the snow
and sunlight is benign on everything;
                                                    Jack found
by pale balloons made of gold beater's skin, found
and then lifted over the daisied snowfields,
dropping his paper messages behind;
                                            Jack as a kind
of flower himself, drifting beneath the pale corolla,
white light coming to him from the ground.

BEECHEY ISLAND, 1850

Three graves. And, left behind,
a pair of cashmere gloves laid out to dry
with stones upon the palms.

John Torrington, underground,
lies in his sea chest with open eyes,
afloat in a bay of ice.

William Baines, John Hartnell
swim on their backs in the permafrost,
the earth grown glaucous

between their pallid fingers
held down with stones, held down with
wood and words:

'Consider your ways';
'Choose ye this day whom ye will serve' —
admonitions from gloved hands.

A cliff, out of middle distance,
presses. The barely-liquid sea slops
just beyond their heels.

And they are glass sailors
under glass, precious in vitrifaction.
A lock of buried hair

snaps off, to ring
in the frozen ground like crystal
fallen from numb fingers.

CLOISTERED

I.

The Essen Madonna challenges with an apple —
one that is warty, wormed with jewels —
saying that she is not like Eve, who bit,
who swallowed.
                    The apple is embossed gold.
Her gold mouth would break against it.
The challenge is virtue. She chooses not to sin,
holding the studded fruit forever in her hand.

2.

He slips, resigned, between the wyvern's jaws
with unprotesting arms slack alongside his body,
legs hardly kicking. Miserere. Thy will be done.
He has abjured the struggle.
                    Meanwhile vitality
drains altogether into the monster's gullet
frilled with oak scallops, folded with gaping
through centuries of insouciant devouring.

THE NEEDLE

Thread me with your long body.

I am the needle.
I am slim and silver in these sheets.

Pull through me
the whole length of you.
My eye is hungry
for your fibre.

I am not dangerous
unless ignored,
left in a fold of linen
where discontent sharpens me.
I hone my point
to punish the careless
who'd leave me lying.
Shine dulls
from rust or dust.

But you —
who searched me out
in the dense hay bale,
turned cliché head down —
use me for proper sewing.

We two,
bones interpenetrative,
flash back and forth
making a precious lace.

THE WOOL-ROOM

This is the women's room
where we fold and roll the fleeces
in a light like milk — come out of wool.
Milk out of women, light from wool.

Scents on our fingers — grass and thyme.
Stink on our fingers — faeces, tar.
The oil in the wool smoothes out the lines
that cross our palms, the fading lines;

for we stand here without history
and turn the leg wool in
— feeling the fleeces stir against our bodies
like sleeping sheep that stretch their bodies —

doing the same as we have always done,
the women in the wool-room:
folding and rolling in our turn,
dying in our turn . . . .

Under the moon the fleeces cool
in light blued like skimmed milk.
Yellow leaks out of them.
Breath leaches out in them.

EUN BAIS

Christine
of the cool cheek
and close-up scent
of violets,
the death bird
pecks at you.

It is all beak,
all arrow,
and it roots
in the cup
of your pelvis
like a sow.

Your face
is a drumskin now.
You are hollow within,
and the **eun bàis,**
death bird,
beats.

PERSEPHONE IN HADES

I.

If I scream
the dark will fill my throat.
That must surely
be the end of me.

It is necessary
to keep the black at bay —
not to breathe in,
not to let part my teeth.

The hollow inner places
are the traitors —
body caverns
emulating this:

so like a maw
a yawn,
a snarl,
a cry,

so like the barren womb,
the starving stomach.
I can be a lantern
until I gape my lips

and dark swarms in
to swamp the flame
borne within me so far
down out of day.

I shall be extinguished
quite —
the self of light
put out.

No breathing in this place,
no speaking,
drinking,
eating . . . .

2.

Six drops of black
slip down
like oil,
like sealed-in seeds

— flavour of vine
or fig tree,
fruit flat
on the southern wall.

The branch of dark
begins
its quiet growth,
finger-spread twigs

edging
within
the bone cave of the chest,
rooted along the thighs.

My lamp is squeezed
by tendrils,
overlaid
with fronds —

I am half
blotted out
already.
Evening

invades
and I am indolent,
faced with the end of light.
It is not so bad

to suck in darkness
thus —
become the fruit
of shade . . . .

DARK CONTINENT

Street lights select their slices of the night,
exposing sudden details, humble under-things,
to us, who ride beside, above them, in the final bus.

Dry jigsawed walling is for a second mossed
exactly as cloisonné. Under the privet hedge
discarded branches plait to pattern in the nether
    glow.

Black cat, experienced from eight deaths died already,
flirts in the light-lake's fringes with ideas
of ends: the bus's rolling wheels as wide as Africa.

NIGHT BUS

You have to hold on to your faith in a world outside;
that, where the road bends here, the thin copse lifts
its fingers of trees in the dark, half shielding the
    field beyond
where three horses always graze, the two dappled, the
    one brown.

For no-one looks in at the window save your own ghost
keeping pace. You press your shoulder up against the
    darkness
that presses its shoulder up against the glass. There
    is nothing
to be seen past dried mud splashes like grey feathers.

And you know there could be anything out there: the bus
is lurching on a knife-edge ridge, precipices right
    and left;
or that you and your companions never left the garage
but wait in a windowless hangar with the engine revved.

MOONDAY, 1969

Stretch-eyed on the Tube from a night without sleeping,
I watch the people — smaller now
the possible world is a globe no longer,
but a pear — in part of air —
catching the moon in its core.

In pale on darker grey the frogman astronaut
tilted to take that step, transferred his weight
from man-made metal to a moon
whose near horizon was a sunstruck blade
behind his moving head.

And everything changed forever.

The greengrocer cries his wares today as
'Strawberries from the moon'. Black cherries
from his box are round and strange,
staining my hands with maps
of lunar shadows.

WITCH-DREAM

1. Of the devil

He is clenched within the shadow of a man
at noon of day in the garden.
He is a black ball rolled into that shade.
I follow after.

He climbs on my lap as a half-grown boy.
He stands on my thighs.
I bend my neck to his nakedness to suck
of the dark-fleshed child.

He has black ribs shiny as lake water,
icy as water to the taste.
I slip through the bars of polished bone.
They hold me fast.

2. Of imps

It is a great field of familiar creatures.
We play here all together, they and I:

'Antony', 'Blackfast', 'Sacke and Sugar' —
rabbits quick-bobbing at my heels;
a cloud of flies that settle to suckle;
cricket that echoes; spider spinning wheels;
cats crouching in the long grass — 'Germany',
'Jackly', 'Newes'; black dog that watches
out of his place of shade.

3. Of the image

Clay baby in the ground, hushabye.
You are home, it is always night now;
the darkness leans your eyelids fast asleep.

They crowd to your shape of earth,
those nurses grazing lips, lullaby-crooners
at work in the ear, their wingcases shaken.

Black mole that rides the rise of loam
lies down alongside you, hands to your heart,
their flesh-pallor slowing you, slowing . . .

and 'Prettyman', 'Daynty' — mice at their customs —
unparcel and carry your clay bones away.
They tidy the dust of your house underground.

4. Of cursing

I am the spin-top's straight spine,
I am fine as a needle tiptoe on its point.
The air begins to round and round me.

I speak to the impetus, whisper inside
this tower of wind that is all ear:
pull down, pull down, scatter about its roots;
root up and fly away with it in your teeth;
the bitten and broken hurl from high places,
drop into dust to muffle my thin feet.

5. Of flying

In his black, loose-folded hand I fly
as in the chimney, ascending a blank shaft.
Shoulder and elbows graze against hot rankness.
Freed yet sustained, I dandle in the sky.

I am white as a root. The moon, competing,
shows less bright than I within his palm.
I jewel the night, I ring his fingers.
I am the worshipped image, dazzling thing

riding with dark's wrist caught between my thighs.
Space, rushing by me, takes my voice
and doubles, doubles, doubles it until
black is small matter clenched inside the cry.

Note: Some material for this poem was taken
from indictments for witchcraft recorded in
south-east England in the seventeenth century.

ALICE

'Following darkness like a dream', I brave the rabbit
  hole,
its drop into such black. Under the bank of winter
  grass,
into the house of roots I fall, behind the call of
  something
going ahead, below — see there, its white scut in the
  gloom.

I cannot find my hand before my face, but hear
the mole's pink fingers out of sight unpicking earth,
setting its grains aside, neat piles to left and right —
sexton at work in evening gloves under an eclipsed
  moon.

Night underground is thickening to a point, the unlit
  air
pressing the unlit soil. This is the matrix for the
  worm,
creature with sealed-shut eyes. Roots stir, the dream
is quickened where I am, white scut now in view back
  of my lids.

CAMERA OBSCURA

We scry,
using the rough white bowl —
in the dark,
passing the handle
one to other.

Men
walk upside down
in water-colour
colours.
The sky

swings through a circle.
I con
the earth
with a
concave eye.

In this dark room
high
in a light-drowned tower,
we lean
on the oar

to steer
the oyster world.
Over the mirror
of mothering shell
both birds and bridges fly.

THE MIST AND MARY LAMB

(For two voices)

From a high hill, over valley a hill as high,
she watches, new today into the countryside
from London houses pressing. Mist lies against
the lowland in its different disguises: faint
as shredded breath in hands and arms of trees

('I blow across my fingers felt air more real
than bones');
        milk heating in a pan to fill with
spaces, milk abruptly curdling in the dish,
egg white, weir foam, the frost, a new-washed
fleece flung down. And underneath — the flash
of water caught by the plummet light in ditches
netting with one another.
        ('And underneath it —
veins in deltas, over transparent deltas of hand
bones; as webs, on air, the blue veins hanging.')

Hidden — the gentle hummocks in the fields
where beasts might have been buried or sheep
laid down to sleep beneath the pelt of grass.
Hidden — the routes and pathways, threads that pass
from hill across to hill, warp of a net

('The coloured blood within').
        Showing are edges
only: sharps of fences, blades of scattered roofs,
a silhouette of hill.
        ('What shows is what I lose,
the easily dispensable: the eyelashes and flying hair,
the peeling garments, shoes, moon ends of fingernails
taken by cutting. What keeps is put inside
and shut away. Closed crystal skull wipes
out the work of eyes.')

                                    Mist conjures with the rest
through drawing and withdrawing; it is there,
half there, is whisked away and never found.
What stands in isolation, framed with cloud,
is tree or cottage from a company, its colours
veiled to pastel in the moving air, its verticals
distorted.
                ('Inside the gypsy ball the visions
smear and shiver, rear then dwindle
to the inner eye. Colours blank out or gather
to brocade — through-threaded by metallic
glimmers: thin water glimpsed, a white hair
in the red. I am the mist; within my head, air
clots and gathers, thickens, pales. A fence explodes
behind my eyebrows, same fence is swallowed
by the wavering brain that cooks chimeras in
its seeming steam. I bring chimeras to the groaning
table and sit down with my knife and fork to eat.
The metal knife blade glimmers among fleeces,
draws its red lines across the white and white . . . .
I pull the mist down on my eyes like blinds.')

Descending from the hill, milk risen past her eyebrows,
held in the net of paths and water, she is seen to
    drown.

A-COURTING SLEEP

I come a-courting, sleep.
Tricked out in white nightgown like a bride,
hair smoothed flat against my neck, I seek
the way to woo you — going ahead down corridors
in the distance, all reluctant to take my kiss,

and I so hungry to taste your own.
This woman dreams sleep's tongue between her lips,
its weight and stillness like a sun-warmed stone
from a pebble beach where the tide comes in and in
in soporific rhythm, opium fume on the foam.

I lie in wait and craft a chance
to meet with you on evening's ballroom floor;
then sit in pushed-back chair unasked to dance,
hands filled redundantly with drying roses,
herbs for our pillow when sleep's drawn at last

to where the scene is set
for consummation: a curtain pulled across the glass,
dim shaded bulb, fresh sheets upon the bed . . . .
Here, on this bank and shoal of night, I pant
to sleep with sleep among the laundered waves.

TERRACOTTA

It is early. The dawn's grey dust lies down on all
   of us
in our edge-to-edge beds. Three boys' heads —
one between his brothers' feet — are darker grey
   stones
upon their pillows. The baby fills the sandwich
of the brick-moulder and I under the counterpane.
I am the potter's daughter. My name is Annie.

And I am quite alone. I breathe a different tune
from all these others. If I draw back in the sheets
I touch none of mine own kin; snailwise I pull
the frills of my edges in, growing smaller but denser
in person. And snailwise I crawl my mind's terracotta
man, the giant fallen image in the grass.

He is inert and warm from the sun or kiln.
I am all tongue on his baked-earth body. Licking
the film of salt like dried-up sweat from between
his fingers, probing his ear or nostril — I come and go
to and fro on the hollow vase, busy in a full
blazing midday. Nobody calls to me to do their bidding.

SLAVEY

One Sunday
I walked out
with a jack of a private
in the grenadiers,
and it cost me two shillings.

I forget
who put me on to it —
that you could get
a man of your own
for a florin —

but I saved up the money
and we met
at the gate of the park,
he in his scarlet
and the high bright boots.

For an hour
we ambled up and down.
The air made me cough
from the fresh of it
where we went

between flowers
and a slice of water;
sun, coming out and in
as trees passed,
shocked the eyes.

There was no talk.
I did not learn his name.
In the scullery
I had forgotten
conversation.

The hour up —
by the park gate
he shook my hand,
then marched away
on noisy feet.

I lay down at dusk
in my attic,
to see damp
on the ceiling
like leaves.

AFTERWARDS

A lifelong affinity with the earth — wet earth
   particularly.
The pleasure of gardening was not setting plants
or sowing seeds, but rubbing the soil with thumb
and fingers, making a damp ball of it, dyeing her hands
reddish grey.
      She understood the people who would talk
of 'mother earth', having felt those arms herself,
having sunk back suddenly against the give
of mud's maternal bosom. All was well there.

Knowing that 'bound to be' was nothing but a veil.
A knife could pierce it easily, a fingernail or brush
   of skirt.
Part way along the drop between before and after,
it was a paper hoop, held out invisibly,
and she had slipped right through it just as a blade
cuts water.
      It made a difference. She was set apart,
and for a long time quite alone in this. Until the one
or two come from the trenches, telling of everybody
dead in the dugout but themselves, or showing
the brass tobacco box distorted by a bullet
meant to have reached the heart. They recognised her,
she knew them, as others cast adrift upon the after.

All uncertainty, all wonder. That the sun
rose in the east again. That on the rock face
underneath the bridge, leaves, that no one but she had
    seen
and lived to tell the story, were intricate with veins
and held the dew.
                        That leaping to intended death
involved no need to plummet. Something would hold
you up, something had held her. Air was a column
fattening the skirt, pressing the legs and stomach.
And she slid down the sky only by inches,
dropped as a feather falls inside a closed-up room.
The birds flew slow and undisturbed below her.

Note: On Friday 8th May 1885 Sarah Ann Henley,
aged 22, survived a leap from Clifton Suspen-
sion Bridge when her skirts acted as a para-
chute and deposited her unharmed in the river
mud 250 feet below. She eventually died in
1948 at the age of 84.

STEPMOTHER IN A BALLOON

A different hawk face in the sky,
dark profile with the sun behind
— imagined from the ground;
really she is too small

and drifting away already.
Her own children run on the grass
in little patterns — the patterns
guessed at on the ground.

The balloon grows and dwarfs,
dwarfs and grows, breathing
red and white dome above
the dot of her in the cradle.

She can look down now,
and see — see everything:
the girl who crouches in the wood
to hide, as well as cattle,

spooked by enormous shadow,
running the slant of the field.
She is an ominous dark angel
with hunched wings in the sky;

and she is nothing, fading
in early-morning horizontal light
and powerless under the weight
of the red and white globe of air.

NANTUCKET ISLAND WIFE

Yellow-white scrimshaw on the mantelpiece,
spider rigging incised on whale teeth,
Nantucket Island wife, her life
an opium-inflated, fish-flecked dream

where only women meet at marketing,
their filmed metallic faces sliding
cheek from cheek, as they incline to greet
their sisters under the poppy and blubber skin.

The meeting house is thick with female breath;
silent she palms the whale that swells her dress,
its hollow core, the blowhole door
that each four years brings her to bed

in unmanned cabin rocked beside brackish pool,
where rising fish break up the mirrored moon
to spider lace; reflection of her face
like yellow metal slippery with dew.

The island turf goes up and down
like sea, like grass beneath the wind the Sound
ripples and slurs. She softly stirs
the laudanum in the glass and lifts it to her mouth,

swallows Leviathan scratched on a white ocean,
glass bell of sky built upward on her tongue,
all that she saw, woman of scrimshaw,
hearing his tales the last time he was home.

JOCASTA: EPITHALAMIUM

Jocasta − queen − bestows her royalty
on Oedipus − a stranger, vanquisher
of the Sphinx.

We stand about and wait for them −
the mismatched pair − though surely gods
will intermingle qualities − his youth,
her stateliness, experience of state,
his strength, so on − so that we do not say,
he is too brash, too wild, she is too old for him.

It is a hurried wedding: hugger-mugger
to the ritual the two must go
− and scarcely introduced.

We clot the palace gate − unformed
formation for the ad hoc occasion −
ready to part − making fresh blotches, blots
in black of shadow, bleach of sun −
once we hear herald cry, they come −
the married, unmatched king and consort.

The difference between them: he −
a high bronze charger, she −
a low, white swan.

Not of their kind, we watch them pace
the palace steps − that long defile
where crowd gaze holds them straight
as stepping down a stripe of light −
until they reach the level earth − our ground −
one turning eyes to eye the other.

JOCASTA ON MARRIAGE

There are three kinds of flesh at least
found in this marriage-bed:
his then — the mottled, crinkle-crankle folded;
his now — the downed, the redolent with sunshine;
and mine between them in the sandwich sheets
— neither as soft as this nor sere as other.

One breed of wedding — that of state —
births all conjunctions, skin collisions:
dry with the sappy and so on. In Laius' bed
I was once young as is my bed-boy now,
who will see me as wattled, liver-spotted
before the bloom of little age is off him.

We make our fruit out of this disparate flesh,
juice that we mill between us in the dark:
metaphor of the membrane sac, the seamless skin
keeping us in together — married — circle word
we carry with us; apple of breath and grape of
    walking,
seeded like a pomegranate with our criss-cross
    looking.

Ripening of it rests with us, rests on us —
sense of a sweetening, reddening through days
after the raw, hard, unexpected tartness
born of mismatching — his velvet bloom to my stone.
We make it other, plump the place around us
within our wedding rondure — readying for the vintage.

THE WEATHER COMING

I.

Out of a long way away — the rain,
dapple of shade on the sea pelt,
tower of cloud to match the tower
I watch from. Weather coming.

2.

Anne Mowbray's unearthed skull
with fallen jaw, stiff moss of hair
that turns to coral on the cheekbones,
temples. That too a certain squall.